# A Note to Parents and Teachers

The *Dorling Kindersley Readers* series is a reading program for children that is highly respected by teachers and educators around the world. The LEGO Group has a global reputation for offering high quality, innovative products, specially designed to stimulate a child's creativity and development through play.

Now Dorling Kindersley has joined forces with the LEGO Group to produce the first-ever graded reading program based around LEGO play themes. Each *Dorling Kindersley Reader* is guaranteed to capture a child's imagination, while developing his or her reading skills, general knowledge, and love of reading.

The books are written and designed in conjunction with literacy experts, including Linda Gambrell, the Director of the School of Education at Clemson University.

Linda Gambrell has served as an elected member on the Board of Directors of the International Reading Association and has acted as President of the National Reading Conference.

The four levels of *Dorling Kindersley Readers* are aimed at different reading abilities, enabling you to choose the books that are right for each child.

**Level 1** – Beginning to Read
**Level 2** – Beginning to Read Alone
**Level 3** – Reading Alone
**Level 4** – Proficient Readers

The "normal" age at which a child begins to read can be anywhere from three to eight years old, so these levels are only guidelines.

Dorling **DK** Kindersley

LONDON, NEW YORK, SYDNEY, DELHI, PARIS,
MUNICH and JOHANNESBURG

**Senior Editor** Cynthia O'Neill
**Senior Art Editor** Nick Avery
**Senior Managing Art Editor** Cathy Tincknell
**DTP Designer** Andrew O'Brien
**Production** Nicola Torode
**US Editor** Gary Werner

**Reading Consultant** Linda Gambrell, PhD

First American Edition, 2000

01 02 03 04 05 10 9 8 7 6 5 4 3

Published in the United States by
Dorling Kindersley Publishing, Inc.
95 Madison Avenue
New York, New York 10016

Baxter, Nicola
    Rocket rescue / by Nicola Baxter.--1st American ed
    p. cm. -- (Dorling Kindersley LEGO readers)
    Summary: BB is selected from thousands of candidates to train for
a trip to Mars, but his first mission is into space to give emergency
aid.
    ISBN 0-7894-6701-1 -- ISBN 0-7894-6702-X (pbk)
    [1. Space Flight--Fiction.] I. Title. II. Series.

PZ7.B3377 Ro 2000
[E]--dc21
                                        00-024010

Printed and bound by L Rex, China

The publishers would like to thank the following for their kind
permission to reproduce their photographs:
NASA, pages 7 tr, 11 tr, 15 br, 19 tr, 23 br, 32 tr, cl,
cr, bl and Bob Guthany and the Space & Rocket Center, Alabama,
page 25 tr

**www.dk.com**

DORLING KINDERSLEY *READERS*

# ROCKET
# RESCUE

Written by Nicola Baxter • Illustrated by Julian Baum

A Dorling Kindersley Book

# Whoooosh!

As BB arrived at Space Port,
a rocket zoomed into the sky.
Lights flashed and
scientists hurried to their posts.

It was another busy day
at the space center.

At the Training Station,
BB saw his teacher, Captain Walker.
"Are you ready for
your last day of training, BB?"
asked Captain Walker.
"Yes, Sir!" said BB.

## Astronauts

Astronauts are people who fly into space. They must train and study for years before they make a flight.

He still couldn't believe
that he had won
the Space Port Competition.
Thousands of young people
had entered.
BB had won
first place.
He had won the
chance to train
as an astronaut.

BB had to pass one last test.
Then he could go
on a mission to Mars.
"This machine will show you what
it feels like to travel into space,"
Captain Walker told him.

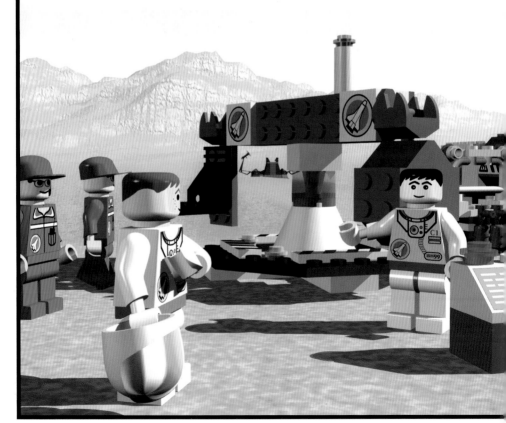

BB climbed inside.
Suddenly, the machine started
spinning around very, very fast.
BB felt strange and
his body felt light.
He was afraid he would be sick.

The machine stopped whizzing around.
At last, BB's head stopped spinning.
"You've passed the test, BB!"
said Captain Walker.
"Come with me to
Mission Control."

## Training machine

Taking off in a rocket is bumpy and stressful! Astronauts train on a special machine to get used to the feeling.

At Mission Control,
Captain Walker started talking to
Don Small, the Head Engineer.
BB looked at the computer screens.
An astronaut called Eena Orbit
was flying to the Moon.
The computers were following
her journey.

Suddenly, a light turned red!
"Captain Walker!" called BB.
"Something is badly wrong
with the Moon rocket!
Come and look at the computer!"

Don Small and Captain Walker
ran to look.

"Call a meeting!" said Don Small.

"Eena is in trouble.

We must act quickly!"

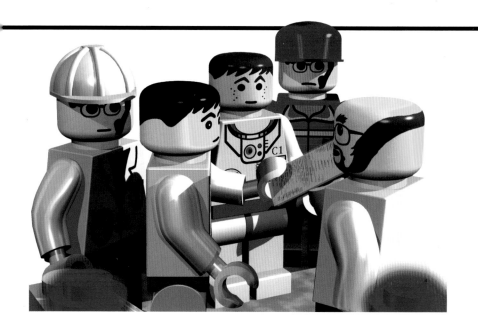

A few moments later,
all the Space Port scientists
were ready to help.
BB wanted to help, too.

**Flight to the Moon**
In 1969, astronauts
walked on the Moon
for the very first time.
They took off from
Earth in a rocket
as tall as a building!

Eena Orbit spoke over the radio.
"Please send help soon," she said.
"A meteor has hit the rocket."

"We must send two astronauts
to help Eena," Don Small said.
"We don't have much time."
"I'll go!" said Captain Walker.
"I can take off right away.
And BB is ready to be my copilot."
BB couldn't believe his ears.

## Meteors

A meteor is a piece of rock floating in space. It can cause lots of damage if it hits a spacecraft.

BB climbed into the space shuttle.
"Ready?" asked Captain Walker.

## Takeoff

Powerful rockets carry a spacecraft into space. They use lots of fuel because they must reach high speeds very quickly.

"Yes, Sir!" BB replied.

His mouth was dry.

His heart was beating fast.

Through his headphones,

he could hear Mission Control.

"Five,
four,
three,
two,
one..."

# "Liftoff!"

A white light filled the cabin
of the spacecraft.
The shuttle left the launch pad
with a roar like thunder.
It shook and rattled
as it went faster and faster.
BB felt light and strange.
It was just like being
on the test machine.
But after only a few minutes,
the shuttle reached space and
the noise stopped.

"There's the rocket!"
said Captain Walker.
He spoke into his radio.
"Come in, Eena!"

Eena's voice was loud and clear.
"The meteor made a hole
in my rocket.
You must reach into the hole
to repair the computer.
I can't leave the controls."
"Are you ready for
your first space walk, BB?"
asked Captain Walker.
"Yes, Sir!" said BB.

**Space walk**
A space walk is when
an astronaut goes
outside a spacecraft
to make repairs or
carry out experiments.

BB put on a special powered backpack.
He opened the hatch and
climbed out of the shuttle.
With one push, he floated
far away from the spacecraft.
All around him, BB saw
the blackness of space and
millions of stars.

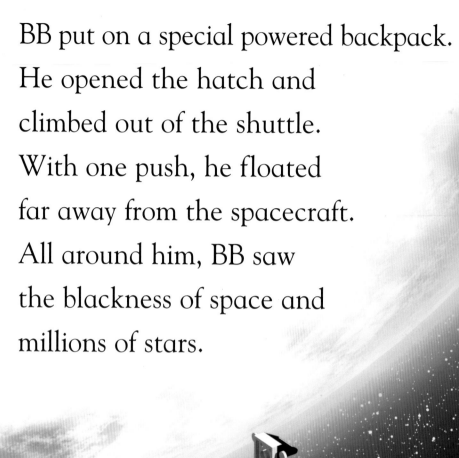

## Spacesuits

Astronauts wear special spacesuits to work outside their spacecraft. The suits keep them warm and help them breathe.

BB floated over to the rocket.
He moved toward the hole
the meteor had made.
His spacesuit felt clumsy
and awkward.

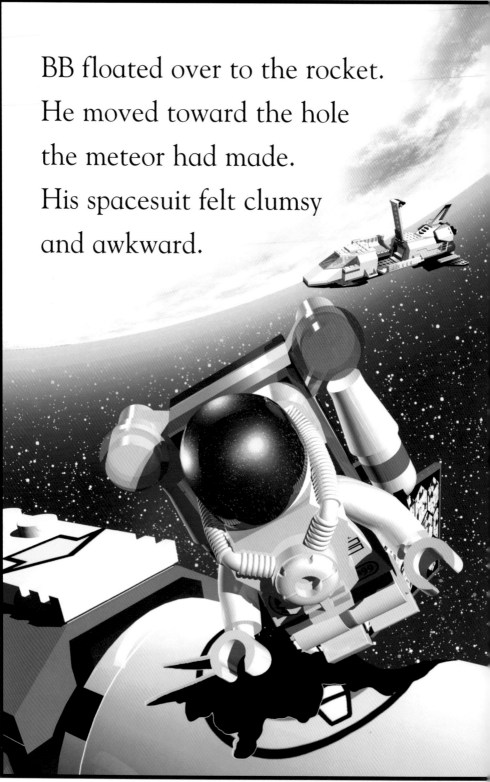

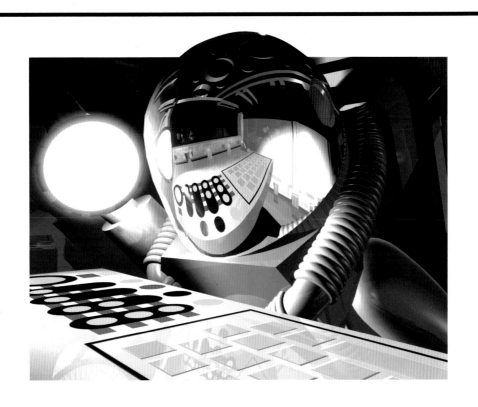

BB switched on his flashlight and went to work on the computer. Luckily, he had come out top in computer class at Space Port.

"How's it going?" Captain Walker asked over the radio.

"I've fixed the computer," said BB. "Now let's see if it works!"

BB held his breath,
as he pushed a switch.
Lights flickered on the screen.
The computer hummed.
It was working!
"You've done it!" said Eena Orbit.
"Well done!" said Captain Walker.

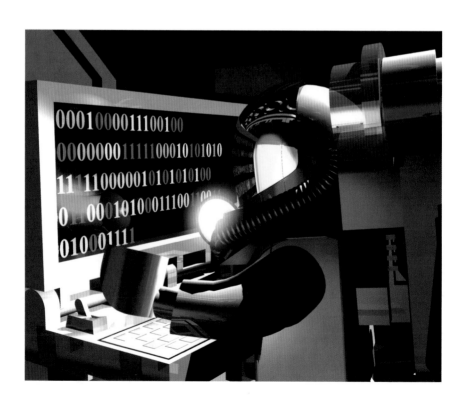

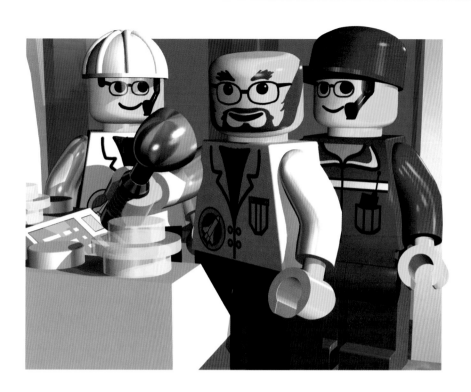

The scientists at Space Port
started to cheer.
The Moon Mission was saved!

**Space travelers**
More than 300 people
have traveled into space.
The astronauts have come
from the US, Europe,
Russia, and Japan.

Back in the shuttle,
BB gave a sigh of relief.
"I didn't think I could do it,"
he told Captain Walker.
"I knew you could!"
said Captain Walker.
"We knew it, too!"
called the Space Port scientists.